BLACKCAP

A RAINFALLEN NOVELLA

BENJAMIN AEVERYN

For Lissy

THE UNHOLY KINGDOM OF MERCIA

32ND YEAR OF THE ROHIT ERA

A LONG TIME AFTER THE RAIN TURNED

1

THE MAN'S BODY DROOPED towards the ground in the breezeless cavern of the city square. The law hadn't given him a hood, so Kade saw the rictus on his face. Twisted and waxy. He'd been guilty, but that hardly seemed to matter anymore. Looking up at the proof of his labour, Kade felt sick to the pit of his stomach.

"You must feel proud, I expect?" Baron Newnham leaned so close he could have rested his aftershave-scented chin on Kade's shoulder. "Saw your name in the paper. The front page, no less. You really must allow me to thank you in a more personal manner. I find money so... detached. We have space for you at dinner?"

"Thank you, Lord Newnham, but evening is a busy time for me." He'd be spending the night in the cheapest bar he could find, sipping whisky till his throat was numb enough to glug it. But the baron didn't know that.

"Of course. A detective's work is never done." The baron blew at his moustache. Not a man used to his hospitality being denied. "It's strange. We lost my sister so long ago... I think everyone had given up hope on the killer being found. Seeing him strung up... well... I feel complicated this afternoon."

"A natural reaction, I'm sure."

Kade felt complicated himself. The relatives of the late Lady Newnham were crammed into the viewing box with him, eyes either wet with grief or sparkling with catharsis. The crowd's chatter echoed off the stone roof above as some threw stale bread at the hanging corpse. Two months of work had led to this moment. The Baron was right, he should feel proud. But he didn't. He felt sick and tired. That man was dead because of him.

There were two killers in that square, and only one wore a noose.

———

The White Dragon hummed with old men mumbling to each other over warming pints of widow ale. It was a gloomy place, even by New London's standards. Even in a city where the sun was blotted out by a great stone ceiling and all light came from burning wick and oil and wax. Candles flickered timidly on the tables, deepening the wrinkles of the pub's patrons.

Sawdust muffled his boots as Kade walked to the bar; guilt muffled his voice as he ordered a glass of cheap whisky. It glugged out the bottle and was too dark by any measure, but he thanked the barman with a nod and took his drink to an out of the way table. The whisky tasted no better than it looked, but it burned brilliantly, and that was all that mattered.

Kade put his head in his hands and sighed. He was trembling. Pathetic. The whisky would soon stop that.

This was the end of it: his career, his life, everything.

For as long as he could remember, Kade had been Father's helper, even though his brother Warren was the eldest. He took notes and trawled through papers. Practised street craft in the gloom. Studied how to read a lie in the corner of a person's mouth.

Now that Father was gone, Kade was one of the sharpest sleuths in the city. But the one thing his father never prepared him for was the consequences of his deductions. He'd never prepared him to face death swinging from a rope.

Snap! That crack of bone echoing in the city square. The straining of taut rope against the wooden construct of the gallows. Sweat pooling in his palms. The dryness in his throat.

Another sip of whisky. Fire all down him, settling this nervous state that had followed him all afternoon.

Snap! Over in a second. He didn't swing for long. A terrible pendulum a murderer makes.

Kade ran a hand through his mess of hair and tugged at the roots.

Snap! All Kade's love for this work ripping out of him. His plans for the future suddenly mute.

Another sip of fire.

Taxes kept rising. They always did. Each year it became more expensive simply to exist in New London, to live under the stone shelter that protected them from the rain-wights. Space here was a finite thing. Kade's savings would last him six weeks. Perhaps two months if he was frugal with food. Without work, he'd lose the house. There were generations of Blackcap memories preserved between those narrow walls. And he, Kade Blackcap, was going to lose it all, cast out from the city to scrounge in some backwater canvas town.

But even with that pressure, he knew couldn't kill another man. Aberrant or not, that murderer had still been human.

Kade's whisky was empty. His throat burned. He got another.

He took out his notebook, his fountain pen, and his bottle of ink. This page was supposed to be for solutions but contained only scribbles in the margins.

There would be some way out. Some line of work he hadn't thought of.

A fresh page, free of scribbles. He jotted down what he'd made in the past year from finding lost pets, trying to work out if it was enough to live on. The total came up short. He added the few stolen goods cases he'd taken. The lone missing person he'd managed to locate. Still short. By a mile. Who was he kidding? There was no work for a sleuth with a weak stomach in a city like New London. Not here, under the stone.

He was finished.

———

Dreams of hangings. Snapping necks. Creaking wood. The excited mumbling of a crowd. Kade sweat through the night. Too much whisky. An anxious night of rolling in a wet slick of guilt, and it had all been too much. When he awoke, he found he'd pissed the bed.

"Fucking hell." He stripped himself and his mattress then threw the soiled sheets and underwear in a bucket to be cleaned later.

Since he couldn't be bothered to heat the stove—and could barely afford the fuel—he cleaned himself with a damp sponge and a sinkful of cold water. It left him shivering, teeth chattering as he towelled himself off. But it was refreshing.

He dressed: plain trousers, shirt collar poking over the top of his woollen jumper, and brown leather boots. Stove still unlit, his breath pluming before him, he finished with a scarf, gloves, and his fedora. Almost grabbed his coat from downstairs, but it felt like a kind of defeat to wear it indoors, so he left it hanging on the rack.

Clean and dressed and head pounding. He was desperate for a cup of tea, but fuck the stove. He kept a flask of vodka in the drawer of his desk, but the thought of more booze made his head swim.

This damn pounding in his head. He rubbed his eyes and temples. Perhaps there was some elixir in the medicine cabinet to numb this persistent banging.

Then a voice, muffled and far away. "Hello? Kade? You in there?"

It wasn't in his head after all. Someone was knocking at the fucking door.

"Yes?" Kade said irritably as he slid back the bolt and let them in.

"By the king, your eyes are red." His brother, standing in the gloomy street in a fitted wool suit. He took off his bowler hat and held it over his stomach.

"Didn't get much sleep. What you doing here, Warren?"

"Well, I know the, uh—" He stumbled as he avoided the word "hanging," found none better, then barrelled on regardless. "I know *yesterday* was difficult for you."

Kade circled his desk and sat heavily, leant his elbows on the paper-strewn slab of oak, slumped his head in his hands. Warren shuffled in. "It was awful."

"I'll bet."

"How's business?"

"Fine." Warren threw his hat on the coat rack.

"It's always fine." Little chance of leading a man to his death as an accountant. Not often, at least.

Warren shrugged. "Whether folks earn high or low, they still need someone to count it."

"And Tilly? She's well?"

Instead of answering, Warren slapped a copy of the New London Gazette on Kade's desk. It was open on the page of his advert. The one he'd paid for the day after he heard the sentencing for the Newnham case.

Blackcap Agency
Lost pets found.

62 Everdon Road

"What the hell is this, Kade?"

"It's a newspaper advert."

"No. An advert is designed to entice people to your business. This is... It's a declaration of defeat."

"I'm diversifying." Kade's fingers found the vodka in his desk drawer. Devious buggers. Well, he supposed a swig wouldn't hurt. It was so cold in that room the vodka was the perfect temperature.

"You're narrowing. You can't make a living from chasing after dogs who've slipped their leash." Warren slumped into the seat opposite, looking defeated. "Is it really that bad?"

"Nightmares. Sweats. Sometimes I feel like I can't breathe. Like the walls are moving on their own, crushing me, squishing me. Booze helps. Except when it doesn't. Except when it makes everything worse."

Warren shook his head. "Father should have prepared you for this."

"Always skirted around it. What could he do though, really? Not normal to react like this, is it? Nobody else has this problem."

"Few get to find out how they'd react."

"Father should have left the business to you."

"I'd have sold it."

"Might be my last option." At least he'd have money to start his new life.

"Is that your plan? Languish here, chasing lost cats until you're forced to sell? Then what? Move to some dirty little canvas town? You'll be dead within a week."

"It's not all that bad out there." Like most New Londoners, Kade's brother had never been beyond the city limits. Kade had. It was how he first got started as a sleuth after Father died, taking the cases nobody else would touch for fear of the outside. For fear of the rainwights. "The journey will be dangerous, but I won't go far. Maybe I'll take up the forge... Wouldn't mind a bit of heat in this weather, eh?"

"You're serious?" Warren folded his arms, furrowed his brow. "You'd really leave?"

"Can't see that I have much choice." Another sip of vodka. His stomach tumbled and moaned, but the pounding in his head settled. Lips blissfully numb.

"And you won't even take adultery cases anymore? Might be able to live off them. Barely."

"What if a jealous partner does something rash with the information I give them? I can't risk it. No... I can't have this happen again."

Warren held out a hand for the flask of vodka. When Kade passed it to him, he screwed on the lid and hid the flask behind his chair. "If you need money…"

Kade shook his head. "What good would it do? The offer's appreciated, but it would only delay the inevitable. If you really want to help, then here." He slid his scribble-filled notebook across the desk.

"What's this?" Warren flicked through the few pages of case notes before he reached Kade's poor attempts to come up with a way for a sleuth to make money without putting anyone to the noose. "Some kind of journal?"

"It's my notebook. I use it for everything."

Warren raised an eyebrow. "Rain take you, Kade. You even have your accounts in here!"

Kade shrugged. "Not much to them."

"How do you live like this? The contents of this notebook should be spread across at least three separate volumes. This isn't any way to stay organised. Not to mention the *ethical* implications of keeping sensitive case notes in the same—"

Kade held up a hand to stop him. "I know, I know. It's a bad habit. I'll try to quit as soon as I've worked through the rest of my bad habits. But in the meantime, do you see any way I can afford to keep up with this damn city tax?"

"What does this say? I can't read your scribbles."

"That one's just a scribble."

"Fantastic. And here?"

"Ignore that. It was a stupid idea."

Warren got his tongue around Kade's scratchy handwriting and sounded it out. "'Mysteries Solved. People Found. Spectres, Monsters, and the Unbelievable Investigated...' Kade, what the fuck?"

"Remember the Boatwright case? Missing child. Father never solved it."

"Never solved it? It was an accident. An odd one, yes, but still... Father closed the case after the body was found floating in the Nene, didn't he?"

"Against my advice. If it had only been the one incident, then yes, an accident. But during the investigation we found a history in the area. That exact bend in the Nene. Seven drownings over two decades. They never published that in the paper."

Warren massaged his chin, brow furrowed in thought. "Two decades, though... that's a fair while."

"For seven 'accidental' drownings? No. That's not long at all." Kade paused, chewed on his next words. "I think it was a grindylow. And it's still there now, living beneath the surface of the water. Skulking around that bend, waiting for children to stray too close."

"Oh, I see. My brother has drunk himself into a stupor."

"No." Kade sighed, massaged his temples in frustration. "This is why I didn't want you to read that one. I knew you wouldn't understand."

"I understand perfectly. But I find it uncompelling."

"Of course you do. You're an accountant." Kade slid down his chair and tried to hook his foot around the flask Warren had placed on the floor. It was just out of reach. "Don't worry, I won't pursue it. I'm already going to lose the house. No point ruining my reputation at the same time."

His brother just shook his head. "At this stage, you may as well try anything."

"Are you serious?"

"Some will laugh at you, it's true. But if you believe this stuff, then there'll be others who do as well. Maybe some who believe it enough to part with their coin. By the king, maybe you're even right." He shrugged. "As you say, you're the sleuth here. Before the rain turned and the rainwights tore down the old world, they'd have been as mythical as any grindylow or sprite. I've heard couriers talk earnestly of being led astray by the giddy flame. Lights sparking off the path. These are folk I trust and respect."

"Unlike me, you mean," Kade interrupted.

Warren cracked a smile. "Exactly."

Kade needed no more convincing. If there was any hope of keeping the old house, he had to try. If it kept him in the city, kept Blackcap Agency alive, then what did it matter if he appeared a little foolish?

2

THE HEADQUARTERS OF THE New London Gazette was situated on the wrong side of the border between Longwell and Town Central. The Gazette was hardly struggling, but the printing presses took up so much space they couldn't afford a more affluent location.

Douglas Inkwell was the editor-in-chief. The man's office was small but well-furnished. He watched Kade in the way a belly-stuffed lynx might eye a sheep. That glint of recognition at the sight of prey, but none of the impetus to pounce.

"Blackcap!" A more energetic welcome than he deserved. "Come to put another, ahem, 'advert' out?"

"Exactly."

"You understand the fee is the same, regardless of whether anyone comes calling? You're purchasing print real estate here."

"I know how to put out a fucking advert."

"Really? Because based on our last interaction, you could have had me fooled."

Kade slumped into the visitor chair, took a folded piece of paper from his pocket and fingered it in his lap. "Do me an ad for the month."

"You know the drill. Penny per word, flat booking fee of a silver. That's per issue, so times it by four."

"That's fine. I've got what I want it to say right here."

Douglas puckered his lips as he read the note.

"And you want this wording? You're sure about this?"

Kade nodded. He was.

"Look, Blackcap, I don't want to pry..."

"Don't then."

Douglas leaned back in his chair, puffed out his cheeks. "Have it your way then. We'll print whatever you pay for, but I can't imagine anyone having use for a"—he squinted at Kade's scribblings—"*spectre* investigated."

"We'll see." Kade got up to leave, checked his coat was tied tight as he braced for the cold of New London's streets. "Gotta try and make the city tax somehow."

———

Waiting was no good for him. Each day passed in an anxious blur. He drank, doodled, drank some more. He lay on the floor, wondering why he never bothered to dust away the cobwebs in the corners of the ceiling. He paced until the creaking floorboards sent him into a rage. He stamped on them until they cracked. He sat beside his cold fireplace with his head in his hands. He tried not to think of the sound of neck bones snapping. And he drank some more.

Time ebbed, then seemed to stutter forward in breathless leaps. For nine days it was two o'clock on Tuesday, then Kade blinked and it was Thursday morning. Acid churned in his stomach. Had he been eating? He couldn't remember. His fingers were numb. Could have been from the cold, or the lack of food, or exhaustion. Could have been from nerves.

After a week, he dragged himself to The White Dragon to eat something proper and try to shatter his strange fugue. The hot pie helped. Steak and kidney and a gravy so rich Kade wished he could pour it over every meal for the rest of his life. It smelled sweet and heavily of thyme. Fragrant and wholesome. His head cleared a little. A glass of whisky, but only a small one. He needed to cut the drink. He knew he did. It wasn't helping. It was making him worse.

Nobody came. A week since his new advert had been printed and still Warren was the lone visitor to his office. He couldn't be the only one questioning the odd shapes that shifted in the dark between the streets. The long shadows that sped under the surface of the rivers. Or perhaps he was. A lone fool in a city of sceptics.

A fortnight passed and still no work. Not a single prospective client.

Feeling defeated, Kade packed away his things. It didn't take long. A hessian bag downstairs. Another upstairs. He'd leave the grandfather clock and his desk with the house. No sense in paying a fortune to cart them into the countryside.

He left his clothes in his wardrobe. It wasn't quite time to leave yet. Another month, perhaps, before he was forced to sell.

Towards the end of the third week after he'd put out his advertisement, his door finally swung open. The bell above pierced the silence with a shrill warning that made him start. It was so early he hadn't opened yet; the door was supposed to be locked. If it was open now, it must have been open all night. Kade had been drinking too much; it was making him careless.

"We're actually closed," he said, finding that now someone had come, he didn't have the energy left to deal with them. It was done. He was packed. Tomorrow he'd put the house on the market. They'd come too late.

The woman froze halfway in. A farmer, judging by her muddy overalls and the paratempa strapped to her back.

"Oh, sorry. W-when do you open?" Her eyes were as bloodshot as Kade's, puffy and purple beneath.

"No, I mean... we're done." He gestured to the packed bag blocking the empty fireplace. "I'm leaving the city."

"But they said you'd help me." Her lower lip trembled.

"Who do you mean?"

"Everyone. The watch. Cline's Agency. Peter Archer. Crook & Simons."

"You've been all over town?" And been turned away by every sleuth. Unsurprising. Few would venture beyond the safety of the city limits. Not for any money.

"I've walked miles, Detective Blackcap." She tugged at the straps that bound her giant umbrella to her back. A thing that size must have been heavy to lug around. "The name's Tiller, but I suppose it's the Widow Tiller now, so you might just call me Penny. My husband's dead."

"I'm sorry for your loss, Penny, but I'm not a detective anymore. My private licence runs out at the end of the month. You're too late."

The farmer's face screwed up, eyes wet, cheeks blotchy. She breathed through her nose in sharp little snorts until she regained her composure. "I'm sorry to bother you then."

Kade waited a moment, expecting her to leave. But she just stood there, arms limp at her sides. "Are you all right?" he asked.

She shook her head, lips tight together.

With a sigh, Kade cracked his neck, made to shuffle some papers, but they were all packed away. The only thing on his desk was his flask of vodka, condensation dripping on the already-stained oak.

"They said you were the person to talk to. That you deal with... *weird stuff* now."

That piqued his interest. "What kind of weird? If you've a murder needs solving, you'll need to convince one of the others."

"It's not murder." Penny shook her head. "It was... something else."

"What makes you say a thing like that?" If her face hadn't been so serious, he'd have thought she was joking. His old curiosity began to stir.

She looked down, fidgeting with her shoulder straps.

Kade leaned back in his chair. The poor woman was desperate. Clearly racked with grief, exhausted, on the verge of delusion. He wanted to help, though he doubted he could. Whether accident or murder had taken her husband, neither were under his purview any longer.

"Sure it wasn't rainwights?" Even under New London's impenetrable stone roof, he'd heard the drumming of rain as he lay awake that morning.

Penny shook her head. "I know what a rainwight attack looks like. He was found in the rain, yes, but... It wasn't them. It's not right."

"Or lynx? Wolves?" Kade ventured weakly.

"If you would just come and see for yourself..."

He chewed his lip, took his hip flask and swigged the cheap vodka inside. Perhaps it could be worth taking a look... But he couldn't shake the suspicion that she was holding something back. "If this is your way of disguising an infidelity case, I won't be happy. And I won't give you a name. I'm not sending anyone else to the noose."

"I promise you. Something unnatural killed my husband. Haven't you heard the stories about the monster in the hills to the south? There's all sorts out there, Blackcap, and no one is doing a thing about it!"

"Kade is fine." He puckered his lips. One look couldn't hurt. Odds were it had been rainwights and she was just mistaken. Or perhaps it was a murder case she was trying to coax him into investigating. Or he'd find it had been a lynx after all. But knowing there was the slightest chance it was more than that was too intriguing to pass up. And besides, he really needed the money.

"Please," Penny said, interrupting his train of thought. "They told me you were the one. You're the only one who can solve a thing like this..."

Kade stretched with a sigh. "You know my rates?"

She nodded. "A crown a day."

"Can't guarantee I can help, but I'll take a look."

"Thank you." She looked as if she might cry. "That's all I ask."

———

New London was a haven. Over a million people, all crammed on top of each other, houses built haphazardly to maximise the space. It was safe and dark beneath the stone. Streetlamps burned perpetually. The roof trapped soot that clung to every surface, coating walls damp and black. Those who lived without the city traded shelter for the sun. For fresh air. For the colour-shifting sky: blue for safety, grey for danger.

Each step towards the city's awning felt heavier than the last. The light from the streetlamps spread in viscous pools that slowed Kade's gait. He pulled up the collar of his long woollen coat and adjusted his fedora. They were in the tail of a cold winter, but today the streets were especially brisk.

They passed through Everdon, heading southwards and slightly to the west. Through Canons Cloister. Then into Cullers Pass. This was the closest to the city limits Kade had been in over a year, and he didn't relish the thought of the trip. Without warning, they turned a corner onto an open stretch that led to the city's edge. Sunlight stained the paving.

The stone of those end houses would be marked by rain-wight claws. Even the streetlamps continued all the way down the road, though the last of them barely needed to be lit with all the sunlight streaming in. New London was bursting from its confinement. There were rumours there was already a canvas favela growing on the north side. It would only be so long before the entire city was enveloped in a moat of canvas and old, rotting iron sheets as the poorest struggled to hang on to their place in the city.

But for now, New London was contained. The edge was abrupt, as if some giant had sliced it with a knife. Paved road ended in a green carpet of grass. And there, the sky, larger than comprehension.

"You've been out the city before?" Penny asked.

"Not for a while."

Up to the last streetlamp. To the edge. Wispy white tendrils coiled through the sky. Clouds. Kade knew they weren't rainclouds, but the sight of them made his stomach tighten all the same. Truly he was mad for this. A trip beyond the safety of the city for nought but the delirium of a freshly widowed farmer. To inspect a corpse and rule, yes, it was rainwights that took him after all.

Something in his expression must have given away his thoughts because Penny tapped the paratempa on her back and said, "Don't worry. I've this for emergencies."

There were people watching now. Eyes at windows. Some even left their houses, stood in their doorways clutching cups of tea, or their own hearts, and watched with an eager kind of horror.

For some reason, the audience gave Kade a rush of courage.

Grass crunched beneath his feet. The sound was oddly satisfying. Wind blew fresh and bitter. His cheeks stung but he didn't mind. His heart drummed madly.

There he was, outside the safety of New London.

3

FOR THE FIRST FIVE minutes, Kade felt oddly off balance. Everything was too far away. The landscape warped as his eyes adjusted to the light and distance. Wind whipped like the backhand of a drunken smith. They walked two miles before his eyes stopped stinging.

"Always pitied you city folk," Penny said. "Especially in the capital. Don't know what you're missing. Tip that hat back and feel the sun a moment."

He did so, shutting his eyes against the glare. The reverse of his eyelids glowed red. The sensation was warming, somehow invigorating. Reminded Kade of that first sip of ale after a day's work. Filling.

"Spend long enough in the gloom, you forget to miss the sun," he said, breathing deeply to savour the freshness of the air.

"There's a canvas town southeast a ways. They've a farrier, smith, tailor. Three cobblers, if you'll believe it. But no watchmen. No sleuths. Nobody who knows a clue when they set their eye on it. Wasn't sure I'd find anyone in the capital willing to leave. Almost gave up before I heard your name."

"Most like to pretend the world ends at New London's awning. Many even fear the sun when it comes slinking in. But I thought you came to me to hunt a monster, not because I was the only one who'd leave the city."

Penny turned her head aside but couldn't hide the flushing of her cheeks. Kade had caught her out. He wondered if he should turn around. No sense in risking this trip if there was no case at the end of it.

"It's not like that," Penny said. "I promise. Being honest with you, I was looking for anyone who'd come. Didn't know a type like you existed. Figured a sleuth's a sleuth."

"I'm trying something new," Kade told her.

"I know about the Newnham case," she said. Kade tensed. "Seemed nobody could recommend you without mentioning it."

"And what else did they say? That I had some kind of breakdown, I suppose?"

"That's about it, yeah."

"Don't understand why it's so strange to regret a man's death. I'm just trying to find work that doesn't hurt people."

"By hunting fairy tales?"

"You're the one who hired me."

Penny came to such an abrupt stop that Kade walked on several paces without her. Her cheeks paled. She stared ahead at a farmhouse that had emerged from behind a row of trees. They had arrived at her home.

A large building of thick wooden planks. Longer than it was wide. Unlike the houses in New London, it had no floors above the ground, and the roof was thick grey-golden thatch. A canvas shelter covered the structure, extending a handful of metres out from the roof. It continued in places as a sheltered path that led to low barns for some kind of livestock.

"What is it you raise here?" Kade asked, half curious and half wanting to distract her from the fact that he was about to inspect the body of her dead husband.

"Swine. Andrew's father added them. Before that it was only the flax." Her voice caught on the last word. She crouched, put her hands around her head, breathing in ragged gasps. "I'm sorry."

Not knowing what to do, Kade put a hand on the back of her shoulders.

"It's a difficult day. You don't have to come any further."

It was hitting her now. All the grief her adrenaline had held back, the plummeting sense of loss she'd kept at bay with marching feet and a sense of purpose. Kade knew how she was feeling, or at least close enough to make a sideways guess. After Father passed, he worked non-stop for two days before collapsing into a bleary-eyed mess and slipping into the most twisted sleep of his life. When he awoke, there'd been a blotchy rash on his face from the tears.

Better to get it out now. Grief won't heal till you let the wound.

"You stay here, Penny. I won't be long."

"He's out... He's... He's outside." Penny's voice was rough as two sticks rubbed together. "He... Under the shelter. But it's not right." She looked up then, eyes fierce red. "It's not."

"I'll take a good look. I promise."

Up towards the farmhouse. The morning frost was thawing now, and the air smelled damp. It had rained through the night. The winter air had frozen the rain after it fell, but now the sun was melting it. Kade felt a little uncomfortable knowing he was walking over rain. That the mud squelching around his boots was wet with water from the sky. He knew it wasn't possible for a rainwight to rise up out of the ground, but his heart sped all the same.

Arriving from the rear of the farmhouse, he circled slowly towards the front, keeping his eyes peeled for anything out of the ordinary. Water dripped in a stream from the sagging canvas awning. He must have imagined it, but for a moment he thought he spied the shape of a single finger form in the stuttering of the water.

No... it had only been the wind rustling the canvas.

There was the body of Penny's husband. She'd called him Andrew; that would make him Andrew Tiller. The canvas panel above him was torn and tattered and flapping limply in the breeze. Blood smudged around him. The wounds certainly looked like the work of rainwights, as far as Kade knew what to expect. Slashes and bite marks. Bits of flesh torn away. Except, what were those bruises on his otherwise unmarked wrist? Perfectly circular. Red suns with yellow crowns. They didn't look like finger marks from the rough grip of rainwights.

There was a line where the mud had thawed. An imprint. Kade bent over, squinting against the sun. Drag marks. Distorted by the rain but undeniable. Someone had pulled him under the canopy. Now that was interesting.

So he hadn't been alone. Again, Kade had to consider the possibility that he'd been brought here under false pretences. That Penny, knowing no other sleuth would leave the capital, spun a story of monsters to trick him into investigating her husband's infidelity... Strange, though, for a man to meet his mistress on his own land, in the middle of the night, in winter.

Kade tried to picture them out there when the rain came down. This unknown person could have dragged Andrew under the farmhouse's awning. Probably thought they'd be safe, but the storm tore through the canvas. No, that didn't make sense. If rain had come on suddenly, there should have been two bodies. He'd heard stories of farmers being killed before they could even spring their paratempas.

With all the walking she'd done, Penny couldn't have found Andrew's body less than four hours ago. This field would have been dark at that time. Even now the sunlight was a limp thing, sheets of red unspooling with little warmth. Farmers are known to rise early, but what the fuck was he doing out here with someone else in the middle of the night? What possible reason could he have had to be walking around outside the safety of their canopy, at four in the morning, with a storm brewing above?

Kade scratched the stubble on his chin, feeling a headache coming on.

There were boot prints in the mud, but they were smudged and ill-defined. Impossible to tell which were his or Penny's, let alone trying to work out the movements of people in the night. This part of the farm was well-trodden. Half of these prints could have been from the past few days. He followed the drag marks back to where they began. Flecks of pink in the mud. Blood diluted with water. And boot prints here too.

Someone had definitely been with Andrew when he died. Perhaps tried to save him, then left him in the rain. But why the one body? There were stories of rainwights stealing children to turn into more of their kind, but if the second person had been taken by the storm, why weren't there any other drag marks?

The longer Kade surveyed the scene, the less sense it seemed to make. This might not have been the work of a monster, but there was something strange about it all the same.

Returning to the body, his stomach sank as he realised he better do a pocket check. Andrew's clothes were damp from blood and rain. The first pocket was empty, but the second contained a folded slip of paper. A note. Kade withdrew it carefully, unfolded it with steady hands, but its secrets were already lost, the ink washed away, the paper disintegrating.

He took the dead man's wrist, sniffed his fingers. Beneath the must of rain lay an astringent scent he wished he didn't recognise. Andrew Tiller had been with a woman last night.

Kade stood, brushed his hands on his coat. For a moment he surveyed the scene, putting everything together. Adultery, then. Possibly murder. Everything he'd vowed to no longer investigate. His gut told him to apologise to Penny and make his leave, trudge back to the capital and finish the paperwork to put 62 Everdon Road on the market. This was a waste of time. It had been a mistake to come. But when he returned to Penny, he found himself asking, "What makes you say monster?"

She'd regained some of her composure, though her cheeks and eyes were blotchy and purpled. More than anything, the woman looked tired. "Rainwights don't drag a fellow under a canopy to finish eating him."

So she'd noticed the drag marks too. That meant she'd taken a close look.

"That's how you read it? Some... 'monster' was eating him? Started to rain, so it dragged him under the canvas, but then the rainwights tore the panel down, and this creature scarpered?"

She nodded, hugging her arms to her chest. "That's how it looks to me."

Seemed a stretch, even by the superstitions of country folk. More likely she suspected her husband of infidelity and figured the scene of the death was just strange enough to believably blame it on some creature beyond the natural.

Still, those bruises on his arm weren't the touch of lover or rainwight...

"Were you and your husband intimate last night?"

She blinked, blindsided. When she opened her mouth, it took several seconds before any sound came out. "That's a very personal question. Some folk might call it abusive to ask a new widow such a thing."

"It's for the investigation. Certain monsters are drawn to the aura of sexuality." A lie, though he thought it sounded good. The kind of thing you'd read in an old story.

"Oh... Of course. Yes, that makes sense. No, we didn't. We don't... It would be unusual if we had." Her cheeks flushed red as the horizon, eyes newly wet. This wasn't a part of the job Kade enjoyed, but it had to be done.

Except... did it? This case wasn't safe. He'd suspected as much to begin with, but seeing the scene confirmed it. Whatever the truth was behind Andrew Tiller's death, there was little chance the investigation would end without the danger of bloodshed.

Snapping neckbones echoed in his mind.

This wasn't safe.

But he couldn't shake this curiosity. The case had its hooks in him. Had Penny known her husband had been having an affair? Where was the other woman if they'd been together when the rain fell? Kade studied Penny's face, searching for signs of subterfuge. She could have killed her husband and laid him out to make it look like a rainwight attack. Maybe she'd hired Kade to track down his mistress so she could kill her too.

Leave it be. He couldn't send anyone else to the hangman.

It was an accident. That was all. A strange accident and a case of infidelity that was better left buried.

"I'll make a visit to the neighbours, I think," he said, keeping his voice casual. "Try to get you some help. No good for you to bury him alone. I'll ask around while I'm at it. Maybe someone saw something."

"Thank you." And she was crying softly now, gripping her arms with eagle claws and trying not to shake.

4

THE FIRST FARMHOUSE KADE stopped at belonged to a family of shepherds. Two young lads herded sheep with the aid of black and white dogs that shot like arrows through the fields. Inside, their mother tended the stove while their father sewed a tear in an ancient coat. None had seen or heard a thing in the night save for the wailing of the storm.

"It were at three it came down," one of the young lads told him, elbows leant on a wooden fence. "Woke me up, it did. Fetched myself a glass of milk, warmed it on the small stove. Da's old clock donged thrice while I sat and drank. Never did get back to sleep."

After Kade explained what had happened, the parents left to help Penny while the lads continued working their flock.

The next farm was owned by the Ackermans. They kept no livestock, save the mass of chickens that roamed unattended around their barns. The man who greeted him introduced himself as Paul, told him they grew potatoes, carrots, swedes. Most of their fields lay fallow for winter.

"Come in, come through," Paul said, ushering him into his farmhouse. The outside was fortified with wooden barricades, but from inside he saw the original structure was one of stacked stones. A fire blazed in a massive hearth. Kade gagged for air in his coat and hat; he undid his top three buttons.

The rest of Paul's family greeted him in the farmhouse. Mrs Ackerman was in the middle of cleaning their pantry, bottles and pots and little wooden boxes scattered on the floor while she scrubbed and dusted. A woman in her mid-twenties—a little younger than Kade, maybe—sat in an armchair near the hearth, plucking at a fiddle. The tune was quick in tempo, but relaxed in tone. Like a mountain stream, falling and flowing over water-smooth stones. A young boy, barely old enough to speak, tottered around chaotically, burbling and smacking a homemade doll against every surface he could find. A teenage girl sat crocheting in front of the fire, somehow immune to the heat, nodding to the rhythm of the fiddle.

"Sorry about the heat," Paul said. "Mina can't practise in the cold."

"I'm sick of the cold by now," Kade told him. "How many generations am I seeing?"

Paul gave a good-natured laugh. "They're all ours. Nearly ten years between each. Guess that's just how it was meant to be for us. Kinda thing they'd call a blessing in the north, I suppose."

"What's this, Paul?" Mrs Ackerman asked.

"Ah, that's my wife, Gemma," Paul said, still talking to Kade.

"But it'll be Mrs Ackerman to strangers," she said.

"With the fiddle is Mina, our eldest. By the fire's little Gem. And this little monster's Tomtom." He chased his youngest, tickled him under the armpits, sent the boy giggling and burping and rolling on the floor.

"Leave him be," Mrs Ackerman snapped. "You'll make him dizzy, and I've just cleaned that floor!"

Paul flashed Kade a guilty smile, went to his wife's side, rubbed her back.

"Sorry to ambush you with strangers while you're working so hard, love. Only, this gentleman's from the city, you know, and he's come with dire news."

The fiddle stopped. Five Ackermans all stared at him, waiting for some explanation.

Kade took off his hat, threw it on the coat rack by the door, pushed back his mussed-up hair. "Not sure it's suitable for the young ones."

"Oh, pish posh," Mrs Ackerman waved his words away. "We're country folk."

"Very well. Your neighbour, Andrew Tiller, was found dead this morning."

He scanned their faces. False worry. Confusion. The vacancy of youth. Then there was Mina. Her eyes stretched a little too wide. Her lips parted. She made to put her fiddle down, but her hands were suddenly clumsy and she dropped it with a clatter.

"Oh, poor Penny," Mrs Ackerman said, drawing Kade's attention. He flicked his eyes back to Mina, but in that moment she'd found her composure. She now wore the most believable expression of neighbourly concern. "Suppose she needs some strong arms to dig, eh? Maybe someone who knows some old words to say over the grave?"

"I'm sure she'd appreciate both," Kade said. "While I'm here, none of you happened to notice anything strange last night?"

"Don't notice much when I'm sleeping."

"It rained awful hard," Gem said, her crotchet abandoned in her lap.

"Yes." Kade nodded. "It looks like a terrible accident. But it's my job to ask questions, so I do."

Mrs Ackerman narrowed her eyes, catching on. "You're a sleuth."

"Penny came to me this morning. A natural reaction when there's a sudden death like this—even if it's obvious the rain got him."

"You better not take her money. She weren't in her right mind if she hired a sleuth for a rainwight attack." She clapped her hands and Kade almost jumped. "Right then. We all better be off. Get Tomtom's coat on him, will you, Gem? Mina, put that fiddle away properly!"

"I might stay, actually," Mina said. "Keep the fire going."

"You can look after the little one, then."

As the Ackermans prepared to leave, Kade made some excuse about visiting the next farm and made his exit.

Instead of leaving, he circled around behind one of their barns, gave a brown chicken a scratch on the head, counted enough seconds to make it two minutes, then trudged back to the farmhouse and knocked on the door. No answer. He knocked again.

The door opened a crack and one of Mina's eyes blinked at him through it.

"My parents have left for the Tillers', Mr Sleuth."

"It's Kade. And I'm afraid I left my hat." He ruffled his naked hair to illustrate his point. The door didn't budge. "If you don't want to let me in, just pass it out."

She scrambled behind the door for a moment, then opened it further to shove his hat to him. Before she had a chance to close the door, he said, "Did you know Andrew Tiller well?"

"What? What do you mean?" She bowed her head, clearly shy. Or nervous.

"Looked awful cut-up to hear about his death."

"He was a good neighbour."

"See much of him?"

"I really should be watching Tomtom."

"Handsome man for his age, huh?" Not that Kade had been able to tell from the state of his corpse.

"Wouldn't really know." She paused and looked off to the side, as if remembering something. "Guess you could say I was fond of him. He helped me once."

"I don't want to press you too hard, but would you mind telling me what he helped you with?"

"My parents don't know, you see."

"I won't tell them. Won't tell his widow neither, if that's a worry for you."

Mina shook her head. "Wouldn't be nothing like that." She sighed, perhaps realising it was worse to leave him speculating than to spill the truth. She leaned closer to the gap in the door, whispered as if there was any chance of little Tomtom understanding what she was saying. "Friend of a friend works in the city. In a hospital. Sometimes she tampers with the books to make a bottle of laudanum spare and it ends up in her pocket. We have little parties where it all gets drunk—it's not a regular thing, you understand. One time she brought this powder instead. You put it up your nose. On the back of your hand, then a big sniff. Made me feel strange. Didn't like it. I came running home and didn't even notice it was spitting rain. Ran straight to the Tillers'. Thank the king that I made it before the rainwights formed. Andrew took me in, made me a hot tea of calming herbs that fixed me up some. Never told anyone about it. Never told my parents how stupid I'd been. So, yeah, it was a shock to hear... He was a good man. One that didn't deserve to go that way."

"His wife wasn't home? When he took you in, I mean."

Mina shook her head. "Were at the Royal Market. Got stranded by the rain. By the time she got back, I was gone. You won't tell Mrs Tiller, will you? She's as good a lady as you'll find and I wouldn't want her to get the wrong idea."

"Don't worry, you're fine."

"Well, now. You've got your hat." And with that, she slammed the door.

As he walked away from the Ackermans' farmhouse, Kade wondered how much of Mina's story was true. Most of it, perhaps. The best lies are composed mostly of truth. But she'd been overly nervous. Her reaction to Andrew's death lingered with him. It could have been a flicker of grief. Or of guilt. Was she afraid he was somehow onto her?

If he kept pulling at this thread, he was going to unravel something he didn't want any part in. Adultery. Murder. Conspiracy. Penny lured him out there with tales of monsters, but if he stuck with the case, someone was going to end up dead. Or hurt. He could feel it. Mina, or Penny, or some other player. Whether they were guilty or not, he couldn't be responsible for causing another person harm. Not again.

When he returned to the widow's farm, he made his excuses as best he could.

"I don't think there's a case here. Not one I can work, at least."

"What do you mean no case?" she snapped. "My husband's dead, isn't he?"

Kade shrugged, feeling wretched. Penny needed to sleep off some of her grief, give the shock of it time to settle. But he wasn't going to be the one to tell her so.

"Looks like an accident to me. A slightly odd one, true, but no more than that. There's a risk to living and working out here in the open air. You know that."

As he walked away, she called after him, "But what about the monster, detective? It's still out there!"

"If there's really such a thing, then I'm no use to you anyway." He carried on walking, tugging down the brim of his fedora and pulling his collar close around his neck. "I'm only good for finding lost pets."

5

"Do you have any idea how much a forge costs?" Warren tapped the page in his journal he'd dedicated to proving how hopeless Kade's prospects were. "Plus, you need hammer, anvil, chisel."

"Why do I need a chisel to work iron?"

"You see? How can you compete with folks who started training when they still had one thumb in their mouths?"

Kade pursed his lips, sipped his pint. Warren had insisted on taking him somewhere nicer than The White Dragon. He was paying. Whatever fuel filled the lamps on the walls burned white and flickered energetically.

"It was only an idea."

"But do you have another? Because you don't have long left to sell Father's old house before you'll be forced to start paying city tax out of the value of the house itself, and once you get the banks involved, you're fucked." He took a hearty swig of his cloudy cider; too sweet for Kade. "That's my professional opinion, by the way."

"You're too drunk to have a professional opinion right now."

"Money"—Warren leaned closer, rubbing his fingers together—"is leaking out of your eyeballs, brother. And the banks won't hesitate to lap it up."

"Most disgusting metaphor you've used this week."

Warren leaned back in his seat, face sobering. "But really, you need a plan. I've seen people fall before, Kade. There's a point of no return. Can't move to a canvas town if you've no money for a house."

"Can always build one with my own hands."

"You think too much of your own capabilities. You can't even make it work as a sleuth, and that's the one thing you're actually trained for!"

"Hey!" Kade jabbed a finger on the table. "I'm a damn good detective. You know that's not the problem."

"Sure, sure." Warren waved dismissively. "Took a case the other day, though, eh? Where's the money from that?"

"Didn't feel right. Someone was gonna get hurt if I kept asking questions."

"It didn't feel right. Of course. That job could have bought you an extra month to get your affairs in order, but no, it had a weird *feeling,* so you walked away." He threw the latest New London Gazette across the table. The crossword was already filled in. "At least have a look for work in there."

"You get meaner after every drink."

"I have to be mean sometimes. I'm your big brother. It's how I look out for you."

"Nobody asked you to look out for me."

"Father did." He closed his eyes, took a deep breath. "Look, I can lend you a crown or two. Give you a bit of breathing room. But you need to find a permanent solution."

"I'll put the house on the market," Kade said. Warren raised his eyebrows. "I will! You know there's a waiting list. It'll sell before I've left the solicitors. I have time."

"But why the delay? If you're done with the agency, what other recourse do you have?"

"Father loved that house." He rolled the base of his glass on its wicker coaster, fidgeting. "It's where he lived with our mother."

"I know. But they're both gone now."

"Just doesn't seem right to give it up."

"Stop talking yourself in circles and make a decision. Delaying won't make it any easier. If you want to be a beggar, then get on the street. If you want to be a sleuth, then get to work. If you want to embarrass yourself setting up a smithy, or a bakery, or a bloody flower shop, then do it! Do *something*!" The bastard got himself so worked up he finished out of breath. "Truth is, the killer you put down was a nasty piece of work."

"By all accounts."

"Exactly. You saved lives. That's how you have to think of it. By the fucking king, it's how everyone else sees you. As a kind of hero. A small one, maybe, but..." He shrugged as he trailed off.

But Kade still sent a man to his death.

———

Couldn't say he was sober when he made it home. Couldn't say he was even sure he'd let himself into the right house. There were exactly four things in his office: a coat rack, a packed bag, a grandfather clock, and his desk. He walked into every one of them in his effort to find the stairs.

"Fuck it!" Kade caught his knee on the corner of his desk, hissed and nearly fell over.

Everything was blurred, gloomy, spinning. His head felt like it was full of metal marbles all jangling around and *click-clacking* together.

He gave up on the stairs and slumped into the chair behind his desk. His flask wasn't in the drawer where he'd left it. He checked his pockets. Ah, there it was. But when he unscrewed the cap and lifted it to his lips, he found the contents dry. A single drop stained his tongue, taunting him. This was bullshit.

Annoyed, he took out the newspaper Warren had given him. It had been folded messily in his pocket, and now the whole thing was crinkled and sorry-looking. Too dark in there to see the text. Even the bold headlines were just smudges. He lit a wall lamp, unhooked it from its fitting, and somehow carried it to his desk without burning the house down. The flame sputtered in that way that meant the fuel was running low, so he filled it from the reserve he kept in his desk.

"*King Deploys Full Brigade To Repel Northern Invaders!* Hmm."

The war that would never truly start. Over land nobody lived in or cared about. The constant animosity between the Bright Crown of Northumbria and the Unholy Kingdom of Mercia was ephemeral to the point of non-existence. Troops marching this way and that. It was the king's favourite excuse for raising taxes, though, so in that regard, it was the most important conflict of the Rohit Era. It was the reason Kade's place in the city was so tenuous. The reason he was in danger of losing a house that had been with his family since the old world fell.

The top headline on page two wasn't any more useful. And what was he even searching for? Lost pets didn't make the headlines. What else use could he—

"Body Found With Strange Bruises. Watchleader Dismisses Claims Of Poisoning."

Strange bruises... It had barely been a week since Kade inspected the body of Andrew Tiller, but he was so damn drunk it still took him a moment to realise why that sounded familiar.

In a rush, he scanned the rest of the article. A woman had been found by the Stowe Bazaar, near the canal. Dead. Bruises on her arm. Circular. Red in the centre, yellowed at the edges. They were the same markings.

A chill ran down his back. The hairs on his arms stood on end. Unprepared for the adrenaline, it hit him with a wave of nausea, and he had to lean back, breathing heavily. It was several minutes before he felt well enough to look back down at the page again.

The same fucking markings.

He frowned at the article so hard his brow twitched.

With a sinking feeling, he realised he was already laying out the case in his head. A serial killer? But the headline said no poison... It wouldn't be the first time the watch had made a mistake. Or Penny could have been right all along, and this was the work of something he lacked the language to explain. Something monstrous. He shook his head, trying to sober. He was far too drunk for this.

6

IT WAS WITH SOME embarrassment that Kade arrived at the library of the Académie des Sciences Profanes. His cheeks grew hot, imagining the reception clerks could somehow read his intentions in his gait. That the other readers, sitting quietly in pockets of solitude, faces crushed to their books to read in the low light, could guess he was there to engage in the serious study of monsters.

He told himself he was only indulging his curiosity. That he was sure to find some rational explanation for the odd bruises that would dull his interest in the case. He needed to. These deaths weren't safe for him to solve. He had to move on.

Too self-conscious to have a fetcher bring him what he needed, he laboured through the stacks, bamboozled by the esoteric classification system. Eventually he found folk tales, histories, and medical journals from before the rain turned. He didn't know how far back he needed to go to find belief in the arcane, so he pulled the oldest volumes he could find. Writings from long before the old world fell. Stories disregarded as myth.

Kade sat in that library for hours, reading by shielded candlelight. He learned of boggarts, fairies, and merfolk. It wasn't long before he found himself riveted. There was an addictive quality to those old stories. In finding clues he could trace to the modern world. Wizards were a constant. Though in modern parlance, the term was used interchangeably for half-mad herbalists and active con artists. Either way, there was no magic in it. The wizard was who you went to when the doctor had failed you. In the Bright Crown of Northumbria, they had gods to pray to. Down here, in the Unholy Kingdom of Mercia, they had only the fucking wizards.

He found nothing of bruises, but that was fine. Better to find nothing, probably. Perhaps it was some disease. By the king, New London was full of them. Especially in the poorest parts of the city. The darkest streets with the cheapest booze and the sickliest whores.

Yes, better to set this aside and think no more on it.

But then he read of the tooth drinker. The dhampir.

A revenant with a thirst for blood. Canines lengthened and sharpened and hollowed. As the mosquito drew blood through its proboscis, so the tooth drinker made use of its mutated fangs.

He'd heard myths of the vampiric. Of the razor-toothed upyr with their lapping tongues. The shape-shifting strigoi. But only dhampir could have made such bruises with the pressure and suction of their canines.

Perhaps he'd misjudged Penny. She'd had the right of it with her husband's death, and he'd thought she was trying to lure him into exposing her husband's adultery.

Kade read on, not knowing himself if he was seriously entertaining these ideas. Something in the texts excited him. The horror of it. There was a promise implicit in the lore: that these things were evil raised. Shadow-skulking monsters. And they didn't lack for shadows in the lamplit streets of New London.

A case he could solve without fear of the consequences. No man to send to the gallows when you were hunting monsters. His own safety registered only as a practicality to tick off his checklist. He never wore a blade, despite the law allowing it. Perhaps it was time he started.

"I'll take that crown you offered," Kade said when Warren let him into his office. "And another, for that matter."

"Looking for work?"

"Maybe. I need to buy a weapon. A sword or something."

"Rain take you, Kade. One moment you won't touch a case for fear of justice, the next you're asking for a weapon forged for killing."

"For protection."

Kade explained his suspicions about the bruised bodies. When he finished, Warren sat there stroking his unsatisfyingly clean-shaven chin and making an odd *hm-hm* sound at the back of his throat.

"Can't say I find the evidence compelling. But whatever gets you working again, I suppose."

Grumble though he might, Warren fronted the money, and after a confusing conversation with a smith, Kade walked away with a double-edged dagger strapped to his hip, hidden beneath his long coat. He hurried away, eager to escape the black smoke stinging his eyes and choking his lungs. Warren had been right. He'd have made a terrible smith.

That night, he went hunting.

Without a drop of alcohol, there was little chance of sleep, so he prepared himself for a long night of wandering. Before he left, he washed down some willow powder to quell his headache.

The streets of New London were hardly darker at night than in day. Most districts kept the lamps burning at every hour. Certain side streets, markets, or heavily residential areas darkened in the later hours, but for the most part, the capital was a place of perpetual twilight.

Despite the light, walking the streets past the strike of midnight felt eerie. Perhaps it was only because of what he sought. The texts he'd read repeating in the back of his mind. Tooth drinkers conjured by his imagination in twisted forms. Or perhaps it was external. The odd quiet. The emptiness.

Kade hurried his feet towards the Stowe Bazaar. Towards the low growl of chatter. Heavy layers of aroma. Sizzling meat and lavender incense and sharp perfumes. Enveloped in the colours of draped fabrics. Funnelled through the tributaries between the stalls.

It wasn't nearly as busy as it would have been during the daytime, when the market often grew so crowded everyone was shoulder-to-shoulder in a choking press. But it was busy enough to shake that prickling sense of unease. Mostly. Though the thought that a woman had been killed only two streets away lingered in the back of his mind.

Strange that such a dark act could be performed beside such a commotion of colour.

Kade ordered food from a woman tending a stall, then asked, "Seen anything strange?" while she prepared his order. Curried mushrooms and rice wrapped in a sweet pancake.

"Every night." She made a gesture asking if he wanted a white sauce with flecks of green. He shook his head. The same gesture to pickled red cabbage. He nodded.

"I meant something out of the ordinary. Strange for the market, not just strange by general standards."

She shrugged, rolled up his wrap in a single swift motion. As she handed it to him, she said, "No watchman. You a sleuth?"

"Used to be."

"We don't get much trouble here. Rest of the city is bleak enough, eh? Why make trouble in a good place like this?"

"Not looking for trouble. I'm looking for strange."

The market vendor sized him up, brows pulling close with suspicion. "You're here about Carmen."

"That the woman who was killed? Papers didn't give a name."

"Never do if it don't have 'lady' or 'lord' or 'his-fuck-ing-highness' in front of it."

"Doesn't make a difference to me what anyone does or doesn't have in front of their name."

"Easy enough to say when there's a 'detective' in front of yours."

"Not for much longer," Kade said. "Thanks for the food."

The market vendor sniffed and turned to greet the next customer.

There was every chance he was chasing myths out there in the cold. Even if there was a tooth drinker roaming the city, the odds were slim he'd find a clue in that bustle. But even after an hour in the market, studying the patrons, squinting at the humanity in every pair of eyes, he had little interest in returning home. Kade stayed until the cold seeped into his bones and sleep circled him. Then he staggered back reluctantly and collapsed into bed. No strength to get undressed. His first night in weeks without a drop of booze, and still he slept in his clothes.

That was how it went for the next few nights. Prowling like he was a monster of the shadows himself. A dark thing surrounded by noise and colour. His efforts were fruitless, but not once did he bring his flask. That was something, at least. Not much, but something.

———

One morning Kade visited the headquarters of the city watch, hoping to look through their incident reports. So far he knew of two killings, but he guessed there were more. A third crime scene would help him narrow down his search area. Unfortunately, the watch were rarely in a cooperative mood, and that day was no different.

"This is ridiculous," Kade said, trying not to raise his voice. "My licence doesn't expire for another week."

"Far as I'm concerned, you're a civ," the watchleader told him with little relish. "If you've information that can help us do our jobs, then spill. If not, fuck off."

"Not asking for anything that won't be in the papers in a few days anyway."

"You can read about it with everyone else then."

"All I want to know is if you've found another body. One with bruises like the woman you found at the Stowe Bazaar." Because he was getting nowhere with the information he had so far.

"And all I want is to get on with my job. We're here to keep the peace, Blackcap. Not to languish over past crimes. That's your field, not ours."

"So give me the reports..." he said. But the fucker had already wandered off.

It was infuriating. A dead end where there needn't be one. As long as there weren't brawls in the street, the watch considered their work a success, and the sleuths' persistent hunt for justice an annoyance.

Kade spent the rest of the afternoon irritated and restless. The tooth drinker case really had him now. It consumed his waking thoughts. But with only two victims, he had no estimation of the creature's hunting ground. How frequently it attacked. Whether there was any pattern or reason to the killings, beyond the tooth drinker's primal need to feed.

As he made his preparations to leave for the night, he was interrupted by a knock at the door. He yanked it open a touch more violently than intended, still frustrated by his run-in with the watchleader.

"Matthew," he said, proud at how little surprise he gave away in his tone.

"Kade. Are we on first-name terms?" Matthew Crook, one of the most established sleuths in the city. Crook & Simons was a veritable enterprise. Even a passing glance at the bespoke elegance of Crook's grey wool suit was evidence to their success.

"When someone turns up on my doorstep unannounced, I figure we're past formalities."

"If you invite me in, I might agree."

"Do I have to? I'm on the tail end of a four-day hang-over." Or, more likely, he was suffering mild withdrawal.

"Put some tea on and suck it up. This will interest you." Crook pushed past him, briefly took in Kade's spartan office, then draped his scarf over the back of the visitor chair. He kept his hat and jacket on. They were of a finer cut and fabric than anything Kade owned, but it must have been cold walking the streets of New London without a proper coat. Crook did not sit down.

"If you're interested in the building, I'll be putting it up any day now, just keep an eye open." Kade slouched in his chair, went for his flask, found it empty—probably for the best. Crook lit a cigarette, slid a slip of paper across the desk, then folded his arms. "What's this?"

"Watch report."

"I can see that. Where did you get it?"

"We work closely with the City Watch now. An extension of their long arm, if you will. They keep us informed."

Kade unfolded the report and gave it a scan. One dead. Male. Mid-thirties. Cobbler. Strange bruising—not on his wrist, but his neck. Found in an alley off Welton Road five days ago, not far to the southwest. Along with Andrew Tiller to the south, and the woman found east by the Stowe Bazaar, he now had a rough triangulation of the creature's range across the south and east of New London. An area to search.

"How'd you know?" Kade asked, eyeing him suspiciously. Crook played innocent. "Why bring this to me? This isn't a guess. You knew I'd be interested in it."

"I know you've had your troubles, but you're a decent enough detective, Kade."

"Please don't offer me a job."

Crook took a contemplative drag of his cigarette. "Just seems a waste to let you moulder away in some kingforsaken canvas town."

"Answer my question." Kade folded the report, then threw it at him. It pinged off his broad chest and settled on the floor. "Have you been following me?"

"Only your work." He sighed, shoulders slumping. "As I said, I have friends in the watch. One of which overheard your conversation with the watchleader earlier. They thought you might appreciate this."

"And you thought it would make a nice olive branch."

"Doesn't it?"

Kade shrugged. "You know what I'm investigating?"

Crook shuffled his feet, looked down as if he knew but didn't want to say. "You've been hanging around the Stowe Bazaar," he said, darting nimbly around the truth of it.

"And? Think I'm crazy?"

"I was taught never to play with loaded words." Crook grinned weakly. "But some have floated doubts around the, uh, strength of your wit since the Newnham case."

"Warranted, probably. I've not been myself."

"Nevertheless, I wouldn't bet against your analysis. Or your gut." A pause. "Or your wit, for that matter."

"Are you flirting with me, Crook?"

"Oh, I'm sure you're out of my league. Or you would be if you kicked the drink and bought some proper clothes. Besides, I'm fond of fairer types."

Kade stuck his tongue out at the thought of fairer types.

Crook collected his scarf from the back of the chair, swept it back around his neck.

"I suppose I'll leave you to it. To work, or... whatever it is you're doing." Before he left, he turned back and added, "Not that I believe in fairy tales, but if I were you, I'd keep wearing that blade you picked up. Who knows when you might have need of it?"

"You *have* been following me!"

The bell above the door rang as he left.

———

There was no more denying it: Kade was investigating the Tiller case. He was on the trail of a monster. Whether safe or not, he was in far too deep to stop now. It was time to let Penny know.

He found her the morning after Crook's visit, kneeling on fresh-turned earth before a shrine of twisted willow. Daisies and lavender decorated the arch; the shape of it mimicked an old tombstone. Where the stone would have borne its inscription, a pendant hung on a leather thong. A jangle of seashells twisting in the breeze; a rare treasure this far inland.

When he stopped beside her, she brought her chin to her shoulder, eyes tilted towards the floor, offered no greeting.

"I'll take the case," Kade said. He should probably have offered his condolences, said something poignant, but he'd never been any good at that sort of thing. After their father died, he sat with Warren in silence for hours, neither equipped to break their grief down into pieces small enough to fit into words.

"It's been more than two weeks, Kade." She looked up at him with red eyes. Her voice sounded far away.

"I've been working. Researching, asking questions."

"You expect me to pay for work you did on a case you refused?"

"Well, is the offer still there? Do you still want to catch this thing? Do you still want answers?"

"Answers..." A trail of snot hung from her nose; she sniffed, wiped her face on her sleeve like a child might do. "It's taken me this long to be able to grieve. This long for the veil of numbness to slip away. You're poking a wound that's only just begun to bleed... But I'd like to know what you're planning."

"I'm going hunting." He paused. "There was something weird about Andrew's death. I should have believed you."

"Not sure I believed it myself. First few days are a blur. Smudged like oil on glass. I was a wreck." And now she was prosaic and maudlin, though she did seem more... *there* than she had been.

"Well, you were right. Dunno if that means anything, but there it is."

Penny blinked her wet eyes, said, "Thank you. It means a lot, actually. Go on then. I reaffirm my offer. If you believed in me, I'll believe in you."

They spoke for a while longer without saying much. Long pauses between each sentence. The jangling of Andrew's shells made it seem as if he were somehow present, overseeing their conversation. Kade stumbled through some well-meaning platitudes, then excused himself. On his way home, he stopped at the Académie des Sciences Profanes and picked up some further reading material. Then he settled in for a night of planning.

Tomorrow, he was back on the hunt.

7

EVERY FEW STEPS, KADE touched the part of his coat that hid the handle of his dagger. Just checking it was there. It made him feel a touch safer. An unlit hand-lantern swung on the opposite hip—in case he needed to light an alleyway. The night was little colder than the day, but still he tugged his collar up around his neck. His steps echoed.

Every movement made him start. Spiders crawling into cracks in the stone path. Cats slinking into alleyways in search of scraps. Shadows that lengthened and shrank to some ineffable rhythm in his periphery. He walked and listened and peered at every twitching shadow as he made his way east to the canal.

Each kill had been separated by roughly a week. It had only been five days since the cobbler was found. He was early, but that didn't mean the tooth drinker wouldn't be out tonight.

It took an hour to reach the water. Kade half expected to find flecks of blood on the bank, but the stone was clean and smooth. Swans slept with heads tucked into wings. Ducks bundled up in lines like floating pom poms. Veins of green marbled the water's gently flowing surface. There was no sign of any monster. From there he swerved south, a little west, leaving the musty stink of the canal behind.

The capital was too damn large. Even this small section was miles across. Despite the drinking, he wasn't in the worst shape, but after several days of heavy walking, he was starting to feel sluggish. His calves throbbed and he felt trembly. Should have washed some willow powder down with a cup of tea before he left. It was too late now.

Close to New London's awning. The dark crept in as he left the last streetlamp behind. He wandered to the very lip of the stone shelter. To where he could look up at the night sky freckled with stars. The moon was absent.

With a deep breath, he turned back. Marching on. Pain growing, acidic, in his calves. Sweating under his coat even as his hands and face felt chilled as ice. His feet went oddly numb, fizzing with static. After half an hour of cutting north, he needed a rest, but there was nowhere to sit save the cracked pavement. Too far from the parts of the city that never closed. This district was residential. Quiet and barren. So he pressed on, aiming for home. It couldn't have been later than one in the morning. He'd take a short rest, then head out again. A cup of tea was all he needed.

The sound of footsteps caught his ear.

They were muffled. Not on this street, but on one parallel. Steady steps that rang with a pitch too high to be heavy rubber-soled boots like his. Dinner shoes, maybe brogues, or perhaps even heels.

Kade stopped, cocked his head, straining to listen. The footsteps stopped too.

That sent a chill down the back of his neck. Was someone following him?

He carried on walking, set a slow pace, careful to tread quietly so he might hear his shadow on the next street along. The other footsteps picked up again. To test the waters, he stopped suddenly. Silence. The only sound was his own breathing. The cold air went down rough and noisily.

He'd come out here to hunt a monster; now it seemed he was the one being stalked through the night. He had a sudden desperate wish for daytime. The streets felt twisted taut. Stuffed with shadows and silence and air too cold to carry any odour over the heavy stink of damp and soot. His senses were dulled. Seemed counterintuitive that in this emptiness, this straining lack of sensation, he'd worry he might miss the sound of footsteps behind him. But that's how it was. He'd never felt so exposed.

A part of him wanted to sprint for home. To damn the case and run for his life. But he reminded himself what he was here for. There was money at stake, true, and a widow who needed closure. But more than that he had a responsibility. There was a monster loose in the city. He could save lives by putting it down.

Let it believe it was hunting him. He could use that to his advantage.

The mouth of the next alleyway seemed to darken as he approached. A void. Black so thick he could almost touch it. Stepping into that dark felt like sinking his head beneath the surface of soap-clouded bathwater. It dampened his hearing even further, and he could smell nothing save the cold of night.

He broke out into the burning-oil glare of the next street. For a second he blinked, his pupils straining to adjust. He looked left and right. One way, an empty street. The other way, a crouching woman. She was barefoot, wearing a big fur-trimmed coat, hair tied back in the shape of a cinnamon bun.

At Kade's clumsy entrance to the street, the crouching woman looked up. For a moment she didn't move, perhaps surprised he had been reckless enough to come to her. Skin too pale. Eyes wide, shining like there were tiny mirrors behind them. Though she wore a human face, he knew at once she was the beast he sought. From the smile decorated with fangs too long to be teeth. From the feline glint in her eye. From the fact that he recognised her at once as Mina Ackerman, the young woman he'd suspected of having an affair with Andrew Tiller.

"You!" Kade said, rather redundantly, too shocked to manage anything else. She answered with a whistle, a descending songbird tone that broke off abruptly as she pounced.

He braced, arm up. She slammed into him, heavier than expected. Her jaws snapped at his nose, his neck, gnashing and slathering. Fair face turned animalistic. Long fangs, curved and needle-pointed. He remembered how timid she'd been before, how she'd tilted her head down to speak. Not shy; she'd been hiding her fangs.

She had him stumbling backwards, barely staying upright. He cursed himself for not drawing his dagger when he'd had the chance. It was only there, on his belt, but it may as well have been back at his apartment for all he could reach it with both arms occupied keeping the tooth drinker's jaws at bay.

For some reason it crossed his mind to wonder how hungry she was. A week between the other killings; only five days since the last. She certainly didn't feel weak from hunger; perhaps he should have waited. He could no longer remember why he'd thought he could face a monster alone. One that took victims when it pleased.

Even as she snapped at him, he saw the humanity in her face, wondered if she'd been born this way or somehow made. Had Mina Ackerman once been the farmer's girl she appeared to be?

They wrestled, Kade always on the back foot. He twisted, putting pressure on his shoulders, legs back, trying to unlock the strength in those most powerful of his muscles. His arms were pathetically weak, but his legs were strong from walking the long streets of New London. There, something locked in place. She was still the stronger, but he was no longer pedalling back. A moment of control was all he sought. He took a risk, loosened his grip. Mina slashed at his face, hand leaving four red-hot lines on his cheek. But in that moment of inertia, he grabbed his dagger, drew it from its sheath, rammed it into her—

She flew back ten paces, a gust of wind scattering a leaf. They stared at each other. She growled. Kade answered with one of his own. Blood pounded in his temples. The very thing she would drain from him. The pounding was so loud he wondered if she could hear it. If the rhythm of it called to her, hypnotic.

He came at her with the blade. Slash, swipe, slash. And now she darted backwards, less clumsily than he. Somehow she still seemed in control, though he was the one with the momentum.

Great arcs with the blade. His lack of training hardly mattered when his opponent had no weapon of her own. A nick across her collar, where skin wraps taut around bone. A thin line of red. Of blood. So human... Kade faltered, lowering his dagger to point at the ground. Mina was breathing heavily. She touched her collar, brought away a fingertip; a single dark bead. She licked it.

This wasn't right. He couldn't murder a suspect. Couldn't butcher a monster who was nine-tenths human. Who had a family and a warm home and played the violin quite beautifully.

In his moment of hesitation, Mina fled.

Kade sheathed his dagger and gave chase.

Stupid. He shouldn't have hesitated when his life was at stake. If he let her slip away, she'd only come for him again. Perhaps he'd awake with her draining his neck. She knew his name, after all. And his address was printed in the fucking paper. He didn't want to be responsible for taking another life... But sparing a monster couldn't be worth sacrificing his own. It couldn't.

She was quick, bare feet slapping almost silently on the mucky stone. More than once she almost lost him. She took corners recklessly and never faltered. She dived down alleyways, climbed over walls. Faster than Kade could ever hope to be. His breath drew harsh with cold as he panted over a swelling stitch in his side. But he knew the city well. Better than a farmer's girl.

Mina cut through an alleyway heading west towards Fawns where there was a large pond with a bridgeless stream. Kade had no way to cross the water, but she was running fast enough to leap it in a bound. With the stream between them, she'd head south, escape the city into the open night. Clearly that was her plan. But Kade knew a shortcut.

He charged down the street, swung south at the first turning, ignoring the stabbing in his stomach and the wet heat lancing through his calves. Then through an alleyway, onto a main street, broken paving leading out into the dark. Wind howled as it lashed the street, furious it could burrow no further into the city.

Kade barely registered when he passed the final street-lamp. Then out into the open air. It was even colder here. So cold it burned the tip of his nose. His fingers felt numb and suddenly fat as he struggled to draw his dagger. This way, to his right. Not this road. Not the next one... There! That's where she'd emerge if she was travelling south from Fawns.

Kade put his back to the scarred wall of a house that emerged just beyond the lip of the awning. It must be terrifying to live there, with rainwights scratching at your walls each time it rained. At least there were no windows on the outward side of the house.

It was a struggle to catch his breath. His heart drummed in his chest, his neck, behind his ears. Waves of dizziness kept passing through him. Fear came twisted on a river of adrenaline. A ragged fear, cut-glass sharp.

Then he waited. And he listened.

The wind ruffled his coat, tried to snatch his hat, almost hid from him the *pitter-pat* of bare feet on stone. Hurried slaps as she ran for safety, sprinting with all her considerable strength. Speeding for the safety of whatever lair a thing like that kept. Or perhaps simply for her farmhouse and her family and little Tomtom by the fire.

Kade gripped the handle of his dagger more tightly, measured his breathing, tried to calm himself. She grew closer. And then he could hear her breathing too, breath pumping out her nose. She must have passed the final streetlamp. Coming up now towards the awning. He tensed. Braced. Threw himself into the mouth of that street, dagger whipping out in a broad slash.

He fucked the timing.

Where he'd hoped to open her neck with a single swipe of his blade, he instead only struck her chin with his elbow as she slammed into him.

As they fell, he wondered if he'd missed on purpose

They both went tumbling. Grass in his mouth. She yelped and he grunted and her hands scratched at the thick wool of his coat. He'd lost his hat and his head felt oddly naked. As they rolled, the wind tousled his hair. She snapped at him with her little fangs. They almost passed for human. Upper canines elongated bare millimetres beyond the norm. It was the shape of them that was wrong: pointed and hooked. Translucent in the starlight.

When they stopped rolling, Kade was on his back, she above, legs pinning him down. But his dagger was at her heart, tip slid through the buttons of her fur-trimmed coat, the very point pressed just to the right of her sternum. He doubted he had the strength to push it between her ribs. Not from this angle. But its presence gave her pause.

"I looked you up, Blackcap," she said. "You stopped taking cases after the Newnham killer was hanged."

"A monster who reads the papers." Kade tried to bolster his tone with as much confidence as possible, though it was hard to muster from his position on the ground.

"I'm not a monster." She lifted a hand and for a moment he mistook her fingertips for claws. But it was only a trick of the shadows. Long nails, that was all. And one of them broken. She tutted at the sight of it. "You're a hypocrite. You said you'd take no cases that could see folk hanged, yet here you are, stalking me through the night."

He wondered if she even could be hanged. If a noose could snap the neck of a thing like her.

"I didn't know who you were. That you... But it hardly makes a difference now. You killed people and I tracked you down. Can't say either of us wanted an outcome like this, but here we are."

"Here we are," she echoed softly. "I didn't want to hurt anyone." She leaned forward ever so slightly, pressing her chest against the point of his dagger. "Are you going to kill me now? The catcher of the Newnham killer turns monster slayer? Not enough humanity to even deserve a trial?"

Kade didn't answer. He'd let himself unspool this case till he was all tangled in the mess of it. To hunt a monster had seemed no crime. Hadn't expected his monster to have a woman's face with a name and a family who would miss her.

"I don't want to fight..." he said at last. "But how else does this end?"

"We could lay here together until the rain falls and takes us both."

"Your family... are they the same?"

"No! Leave them alone!" For a flash her face was monstrous again, fangs bared. Then she softened. "They don't know. Only Andrew did."

"Of course... It makes sense now. That's why you killed him. I was struggling to understand why you'd hunt so close to home. You nearly gave yourself away."

"Aren't you supposed to be one of the better sleuths in the city? I didn't kill Andrew. I loved him."

Kade's head spun, pounding. By the king, he needed a drink. His grip on his dagger relaxed in his distraction. Mina must have felt the blade slacken. She swiped it aside, grabbed his wrists, slammed him down. Now she was in full control, those long teeth so close to his face.

"I don't understand." How little his voice trembled, betraying none of the fear he felt tightening around his heart.

"If you found me, then others will too. They may already be searching for me. Penny-fucking-Tiller has set her dogs on my scent."

"Can you blame her for hunting the monster that killed her husband?"

She lifted his wrists, slammed them back to the ground. Frosted grass crunched.

"I did not kill him!" Her voice was sibilant with anger. The fear around Kade's heart coiled a little tighter. "What do I do? Tell me how to get out of this!"

Genuine fear in her. She was panicking, desperate. For some reason, she believed he could help her. But she was right to be afraid. Her secret was leaking out unstoppably. Killing him would only hasten the attention in her direction. Crook knew what Kade was hunting. As would the watch.

"Run," was all Kade could think of to say.

"Run where, Detective?"

"As far from here as you can get."

"With you snapping at my heels, no doubt."

He shook his head, much as he was able with how she had him pinned.

"I'm not one to track a monster through the wilds," he said.

She brought those teeth closer then. The tips of their noses touched.

"I am *not*," she said, biting off each word, "a monster."

"Monster. Killer. Either way, there's no place for you here."

"Won't you listen to me?"

"We're talking, aren't we?"

She lessened the iron grip on his wrists. His skin was raw where she'd twisted it.

"It started that night he took me in, made me tea. Don't remember exactly how it happened, but I remember his arms around me. His wife didn't make him happy. Not ever. Weren't her fault, exactly. They dated long ago. Too young. She got pregnant, so they married. Didn't even think on it. But then she lost the baby, and whatever it was between them that had for a time taken the shape of love... it fell apart. Can you imagine, Detective? Marrying for a child that was never even born?"

"I can't." There was little chance of him ever experiencing the same.

"We knew it was wrong. To sneak and lie. Of course that was wrong. But he couldn't bear the thought of casting her out. Where would she have gone? What would she have done? A widow has certain privileges, but a single woman of her age? A divorcée? A farmer with no land to till? She would have been begging on the stinking streets of the capital. Better to hide. Keeping it from her kept their marriage intact. We protected her."

It felt like she wanted him to agree. To vindicate her story. For someone to say, "Yes, you are so right. That was the only way. What an angel's heart you have." But he didn't.

"He knew about me," she continued, eyes wet, lips dry. "I was already… this way when we met. He wanted to keep me safe. Keep me well. So he let me feed as I needed to. We were already meeting in secret. To be together, you understand? What harm was it if I took a sip?

"That night I guess I took too much. He grew faint. Too dizzy to walk. He was fine. He would have been fine… You have to believe me! He sagged in my arms and I dragged him underneath the shelter. What was I to do? I couldn't very well knock on the door and hand him over to his fucking wife, could I! So I scribbled a note, apologising for leaving him and explaining what happened in case he awoke groggy and struggled to remember. I stuffed it in his pocket. I left him. I…"

"And then it rained," Kade said, the horror of what she was confiding becoming clear. "And the canvas tore."

"Never thought that shelter would break." Tears rolled down her face. She started to sniff, shoulders shaking. Her voice grew hoarse. "That section wasn't even old. I checked. I checked the fucking stitching!"

"Sometimes shelters come down. That's just the way of things."

"It's my fault... I didn't kill him, but it's my fault..."

To Kade's surprise, she released his wrists, sat back, giving him space to breathe. Then she climbed off. On all fours, staring at the ground. Her breathing came too quick, each breath chasing the heels of the last.

Kade found himself saying, "Calm yourself," though he knew it wasn't helpful.

"You should kill me," she said as she struggled to control her breathing. "You should. I didn't want to hurt anyone. I never did. I'm not a monster..."

Kade's hand found his dagger. He gripped the handle tight, steadied himself, then sat up.

"I don't think I can."

"I could make you."

He could tell she meant it. "Please don't."

"How else do we make this right?"

He thought on her words a moment. She looked so pathetic. He couldn't help but feel sad for her. The story she'd told was a tragic one. But she was truly a monster. Three dead in as many weeks. And there she was, begging him for a release. Was it really murder to free a thing like that from the snare of life? He could think of it as a kindness.

Mina straightened, took his wrist, guided the point of his blade back to where it had rested between the buttons of her coat.

"Please," she whispered, eyes so human now. Human and wet and red with grief.

"No..." But his voice had lost all confidence. A grim weight settled like an iron mantle about his shoulders as he realised what he had to do. He was starting to realise there was always a price to be paid in this line of work. A price his father had hidden from him effortlessly over the years. He'd been a fool to think he could avoid it by chasing monsters instead of men. But he was here now, and there was no escaping it.

He'd brought this burden upon himself.

8

A LOCK OF HAIR on the table between them. Tied with a neat bow. Almost like a lover's remembrance instead of proof of a monster slain. Penny stared at it with hungry eyes. The corner of her mouth curled up. There was little surprise on her face, confirming what Kade had suspected: she'd known of her husband's affair. He hadn't been hired to find her husband's killer, but to find his lover. The deception made him furious, but he kept it hidden.

"What's this?" she said, playing dumb. And now they danced.

"A lock of hair. From the monster you set me on." Kade kept his voice level, businesslike.

"You don't mean..."

"A tooth drinker. Does that surprise you? Disguised as a human woman. Or perhaps you were expecting that?"

"Won't you tell me what happened? What is this? Why have you brought me *hair*?" Her eyes flicked to the lock of hair, mouth turning in disgust at the golden beauty.

"I want fourteen crowns. Two weeks even."

"I can do you fourteen, but I'll have to fetch it from my safe." Which would probably be a compartment beneath a floorboard, or in her bedframe, or hollowed out of the back of a cupboard.

"I'm in no rush."

"Tell me then." She studied the fading red stripes on his cheek: the claw marks, the fingernail scratches. The curl in her lip wasn't a smile but the priming of anticipation.

Kade told her a version of the past few weeks, omitting most of the details, cutting to the meat of it. He explained how his curiosity was drawn to the idea of the supernatural. How he'd prowled the night, dizzy from sobriety, hunting what he believed to be her husband's killer. When he reached the climax of their conflict, Penny interrupted.

"She pinned you down?" she asked, eyes wide. He nodded. "Didn't you fear for your life?"

"I suppose I did."

"And then?" Breathless. She was enjoying this.

"While she was distracted talking, trying to convince me to let her go, I drove my blade through her chest, pierced her heart. I suppose you'd say I slew the beast."

"Fantastic!" Penny clapped her hands before her chest.

Kade pursed his lips. "Is it?"

"What?"

"I swore to never cause another death... You knew this when you hired me."

"A monster hardly counts." She almost choked on the word.

"Now that everything's said and done, I'm not sure you hired me to hunt a monster at all."

A reddening of her cheeks. Slight, but noticeable. She licked her lips.

"Whatever do you mean?" Too bright, the words rushed.

"Your husband was having an affair. You knew, but you didn't know who with. When you found Andrew dead, you realised he must have been with his mistress. You saw an opportunity. Came to the city to hire a sleuth. Except nobody would venture out the city bounds. Nobody except me, and I wasn't taking adultery cases anymore. But a monster... now that would get my attention."

She fiddled with the hem of her blouse, wouldn't meet his eyes. To her lap, she said, "Someone pulled him under the canopy."

"So you saw the drag marks. Did you check his pockets as well?"

"I didn't dare unfold the note. What did it say?"

"The rain wiped it clear." It would solve nothing to tell her he'd since learned of its contents.

"Will you tell me who?"

"Mina Ackerman."

True shock on her face then. A silent gasp. She waved at the lock of hair as if she wanted to swipe it off the table but was too disgusted to touch it. "The neighbours' daughter? But she's just a girl!"

"Not just a girl. She was a tooth drinker. And now she's gone."

Penny balled her hands in fists at her sides. "That *fucking* man."

"You tricked me, Widow Tiller, into a position I'd vowed not to be in."

"And you'll be paid for it, won't you?" she snapped. "That'll keep the taxman's fingers off your house a while longer. We've both got what we needed."

"You have closure?"

"I have the truth. That's close enough."

That barely deserved the grunt in response Kade gave her.

"I'll admit, I expected more surprise at what I had to tell you."

"I saw the marks on his arms. Sometimes his neck... Not subtle, is it? Just because we never lay didn't mean I was blind to his skin. We lived in the same house. We slept in the same bed. The bastard would come home smelling of sex, but those were no love bites.

"You guessed I hired you thinking only of my husband's infidelity. It's true that was the meat of it. But it was no lie that I suspected a monster. A demon. A witch... Whatever had snared him, I knew it wasn't natural. You say a 'tooth drinker'? It's not a term I know, but it seems clear enough. A feeder in the shape of a young woman. A siren that lured my husband by the tip of his cock and drained him dead and dry! Knowing that she—that *it*—is dead gives me peace. Now I can let my husband's memory go. He can rest. And so can I." A shiver ran from her shoulders to her shaking fists. She took a deep breath through her nose, then her shoulders relaxed. "And so can you." A weak smile. "I'll fetch that money, shall I?"

She left for her bedroom. The sound of shifting wood and scrambling fingers before she returned and dropped a leather purse on the table before him. The coins clinked as they settled. Kade snatched it up, slipped the purse into his pocket. He had no interest in counting the contents.

"Happy now?"

"Happy? No. But at least I'm paid." He stood, brushed the creases out of his coat, adjusted the tilt of his hat. There was nothing left to say, so with a nod, he headed for the door.

As he was leaving, Penny called out, "Blackcap?"

"What now?"

"Why only a lock of hair?"

"Well, I pulled her teeth, but it seemed altogether too gruesome a trophy for a lady."

"I want them." A manic glint in her eyes.

"I promise you don't."

"How awful can teeth be? You did wash them, didn't you?"

With a sigh, Kade produced a small velvet pouch from one of his coat's deep pockets. He threw it to her. It was so light it almost didn't fly, catching on the air though there was no breeze. Penny jumped up to stop it from fluttering clumsily to the floor. He watched her as she peeked inside. The colour drained from her cheeks. She clapped a hand over her mouth, head shaking.

"Right…" she said. "That's quite macabre."

"As I said, it's no trophy for a lady."

"But at least I know the deed is done."

"At least there's that," Kade agreed. "Please never contact me again."

It was immature, but he couldn't resist slamming the door on his way out.

9

"ARE YOU SURE YOUR teeth will grow back?"

"Did she believe you?" Mina asked in return. She looked gaunt and pallid, sitting on the edge of Kade's bed. After he'd brought her back last night, she'd spent an hour in the bathroom, grunting and swearing, before emerging with two bloody fangs in her palm and heavy bags under her eyes.

"I'm sure of it. If she'd been sceptical at first, the teeth convinced her."

"Then I'm glad I pulled them out." The missing teeth didn't affect her speech at all. "They're not really teeth. Not like yours. They were going to fall out on their own soon anyway. See? These are the new ones underneath already." She bared her teeth and Kade saw the stubs of miniature fangs.

"Should have got some rest like I told you to."

"Didn't feel right to sleep." She hugged her arms, still in that fur-trimmed coat of hers. With no fire going, 62 Everdon Road was breath-pluming cold. "Keep thinking of my family. Wish I'd got to say goodbye."

"Do you need... Are you hungry?"

"Not for a couple of days, don't worry. You still have time to change your mind."

"I won't."

"Did she pay? Can you keep the house?"

Kade produced the leather purse Penny had given him, pulled the drawstring, retrieved a single coin from inside. Fourteen crowns. Enough to settle his debts to the taxman. He could even afford to heat this place for a while. And stock his pantry. Perhaps he could repay Warren some of the drinks he owed. "She paid."

"You don't seem certain?"

"Thinking about the house. I wonder if it's better to use the money to relocate. Get a start somewhere else. I'm still no good as a sleuth. Can't live off fourteen crowns forever."

"You saved me. That makes you the best sleuth in the city in my books." She smiled and her teeth barely chattered.

"You'll need a new name. A new way of dressing... We should change your hair too."

"A new me for a new start." She got up and started rifling through Kade's wardrobe. There wasn't much to look through. "Not the worst price to pacify that horrid woman, and the watch, and your fellow sleuths."

"Can't help thinking I drew the attention to you in the first place."

"Once I started hunting again, it was only a matter of time. They would have caught me eventually. You did, after all."

"Mm." Kade wasn't convinced. His head was swirling with doubt and worry. It was cold and he needed a drink.

"Are you worrying about the fact you've invited a killer into your home?" She plucked a shirt from where it hung, held it up against her torso. She looked around for a mirror, but there wasn't one. "How does it look?"

"I'm thinking about a lot of things. Most of them worries." She was still posing with the shirt. It was too big for her. "And it looks fine, if you fancy dressing as a man."

"You don't need to be afraid of me."

"Hard to be afraid of something as benign as a tooth drinker when the taxman's on your back."

"Please don't call me that."

"It's what you are, isn't it?"

"You're a drunk, but I doubt you'd like me saying so."

Kade chewed his lip, hand straying to the pocket he kept his flask in. Empty. The flask was downstairs, in his desk drawer, waiting to be refilled. "Difference is it's not a character flaw to be what you are."

"Maybe not." She put the shirt back in the wardrobe, unbuttoned her coat and shrugged it off. Her bare arms pimpled instantly in the chill. "But I've always had a choice in how I hunt. Can't wash my hands of death."

"Why'd you kill if you didn't have to?"

"I was frightened. Scared of being found out. Of leaving evidence."

"That's not really good enough."

"I told you it's not too late to kick me out."

The clanging of a grandfather clock calling the hour echoed up the stairs: five o'clock.

"There's a pub down the road," Kade said. "They accept all types, drunks and monsters included."

"Go if you want."

"No one will be looking for you there."

She took a jumper from the wardrobe, held it up. A relic from before the rain turned, inherited from Kade's mother, and she from hers. It had always been too small for him, but he hadn't been able to bear the thought of giving it away.

Once brightly coloured, the wool was mostly faded. A drab, pinkish-grey that ignited the gold of her hair.

"Suits you," he said plainly.

"Am I allowed? Whose was it?"

"My mother's. Put it on. Leave your coat. It'll be warm enough in The White Dragon."

They were laughing by the time they made it downstairs. Not wholly relaxed, nor sure of each other's company, but settled at least in the camaraderie of being lost together. Kade reached for the door handle, gripped it, began to turn, when a knocking from the other side made him start. He leapt back, heart galloping.

"Kade?" came his brother's voice. "Are we meeting today? Don't worry about money, I'll get dinner."

"Not today, Warren," Kade said as he opened the door, his heart still skipping. "I'll get them in tonight."

10

KADE'S PURSE WAS LIGHTER after paying off his tax and renewing his licence. Kept counting the coins as if by sleight of hand he could force them to multiply. A month's worth of food and tax. If he wanted to stay in New London, he'd have to find more work. Being pushed to the edge made him realise he couldn't leave the old family home behind. And now he had Mina to think about too.

Another trip to the New London Gazette. Kade paid to run his advertisement for the next month. But an ad in the paper wouldn't be enough on its own.

"How does that look?" he asked Mina as he took a step back from the window to admire the new poster.

"Fine enough, I'd say."

"Think we'll get any business?"

After slightly too long of a pause, she said, "Yeah... might do."

"Guess we can only wait and see."

Nobody came the first day. Or the second. Mina and Kade took to playing chess across his desk to kill time. A better distraction than always reaching for his flask. He was trying to keep a clear head. On the third day, a man barged in so suddenly Mina jumped, scattering chess pieces over the desk and floor.

"Hello? Detective Blackcap?" the man said, eyes wide and wet. The door clicked shut behind him.

"That's me."

He brandished a copy of the New London Gazette. It was open at his advert.

"Nobody else believes me," he said. "I need your help."

———

The time had come.

Kade rolled up his sleeve, offered his arm. Mina seemed nervous. She hesitated, staring at his skin: milky-white from lack of sun. A spot of dribble on her lip. Her chest rose heavily.

"Go on then," he told her.

"It will hurt. A lot. I try to be gentle, but it will hurt."

"I deserve it."

She knelt by his bed, took his arm in her hands. Her fingers were delicate. She breathed deeply through her nose, eyes closed as if his arm were a kidney pie with flaking short-crust pastry. Her grip tightened and a rush of cold ran down his back; his arms pimpled. Kade felt suddenly trapped. He didn't want this anymore. Why had he trapped himself with this predator? This monster?

Her tongue came out, tickled his forearm. Instinctively, he tried to yank it back, but now she had him fast. Those new-grown translucent canines were sharp even as she shifted them lightly over his skin. Searching for the perfect spot. For the vein.

Then a muffled growl. A sharp pain. She clamped down on his arm. By the king, she'd been right to say it would hurt. But it was the discomfort, not the pain, that was the worst of it. Kade's skin tingled. Pressure pulsed through him as blood was sucked up those fangs. He grew cold so fast. Head swimming. He had to get free but he couldn't move. He slumped forward. Her hair smelled of redcurrants. Her shoulders rolled as she fed. For a moment he thought he was going to be sick, but his stomach muscles didn't have the strength to contract. Spinning and spinning. A dark vignette. Then an odd moment of serenity. He strode over a still lake, barefoot in the dark. The cool of night spread through him, breath pluming and snaking and catching at the moonlight. He was in the deep. He was dark. He was numb.

And it was beautiful.

About the Author

Benjamin Aeveryn is an author of SFF from Cambridge, UK, where he lives with his beautiful fiance and a grumpy old cat. Salt in the Wound is his debut novel, but his short fiction has been published by Daily Science Fiction and Almond Press. People say his work is grimdark fantasy, but for a vision of England where it's always raining, infrastructure is crumbling, and nobody trusts their neighbours, he only has to look out of his window.